Inspiration

for writers who don't write,

and want to

Andy Milberg

ISBN (paperback): 979-8-9855210-0-9

ISBN (eBook): 979-8-9855210-1-6

Thank you Johanina Wikoff, Ellen Trabilcy, Michael Koch for your support, all the writers I've read during the past seventy years whose brilliance both intimidated and inspired me, and my fellow writers in the Ajijic Writers Group, who contributed the prompts used in this book.

I'm a writer who doesn't write.

That's how I would have described myself for the past 50 years. Until recently.

What changed ?

I found a writing structure that has taken the pressure off me to produce masterpieces, and reclaimed the joy of turning a blank sheet of paper (or computer screen) into a tangible expression of my creative spirit in the moment.

A little history. As a child I was an avid reader. At some point, for some reason, maybe age 9 or 10, I began to write something that could be called poetry. Fragments that I remember were initially fairly whimsical, then turned to adolescent angst about the state of the world and love as puberty had its way with me.

In 7th grade I entered two poems in the National Scholastics Writing awards contest. A few months later, my school held a special assembly. It was announced that I had won a Certificate of Merit. I was called up to receive the award and applauded by my classmates and parents, who I didn't know were in the back of the room.

Along with my surprise and pride, I was terrified that I would be asked to read the poems, one of which was a love poem about heartbreak. I wasn't, but was later asked to submit it to the school paper. I refused.

The heartbreak was totally fiction. I was 13 years old and already under the influence of family and cultural programming about romantic love. As years passed, love and heartbreak would become regular themes in my writing, based on actual experiences.

Fast forward a few years. I entered college intending to study economics and political science, After a year, I realized I had no interest in either. English literature called to me, especially the Romantic Poets from the early 19th century. Their dramatic, and often tragic lives somehow resonated with me, in spite of my late 20th century middle class American upbringing. Perhaps it was all the social upheaval in the 1960's.

So while I tried to figure out what to do with my life, I would receive occasional flashes of inspiration and write a poem or two. Or journal. Or beginning of something. For the next few decades. Especially when a love affair ended badly for me.

I was a writer who didn't (except occasionally) write.

A quote I read haunted me.

Delacroix wrote "To be a poet at 20 is to be 20. To be a poet at 40 is to be a poet".

Exchange the word "writer" for "poet" and it also works.

I wanted to be a writer and I didn't write. To put it another way, I didn't have the dedication, focus, discipline, or commitment to devote to learning the craft and actually producing anything on a consistent basis.

And I judged myself for that, still feeling the desire to "be a writer" and maintaining the story/identity that I was a writer who doesn't write.

Now, in the year 2021, I'm 73 years old, closer to Life's exit door. What used to take up time in my life has changed in so many ways. What is important has become clearer as time becomes both more limited and precious. Obsolete identities that both delighted and distracted me for decades are fading.

During the past few years, I've been spending most of my time in a small village on the shore of the largest lake in Mexico. Covid hit. A new friend invited me to join a weekly writing group on Zoom.

"It's fun", he said, "At 10am I will email you a prompt, which is usually a couple of words or a phrase. You write for 45 minutes using the prompt, or not. It can be fiction, essay, poetry, or whatever. Then anyone who wants to read does, and the rest of us say only what we liked about what you wrote."

So I decided to try it. Not much risk here, I thought. There's a specific focus to write about and a clear starting and ending time. I'll hear what others do with the same prompt. Seems interesting.

A year and a half later, I can say that it has become both a highlight of my week and a source of inspiration for me to not only write more, but actually organize my writings and put them together into book form, which you are reading right now.

Sometimes I like the prompt, sometimes I don't. Sometimes I like what I write, sometimes I don't. It really doesn't matter. What matters is that I allow the Creative Force inside me to express itself.

And I have let go of the idea that I am a writer that doesn't write.

3 ways to use this book….

1. Read my responses to the prompts. They are arranged in no particular order – some autobiographical, some autobiographical fiction, some pure fiction, etc. – so you can read them sequentially or open randomly.

and/or…

2. I've formatted it to show the prompt on the page before my writing. If you're so inclined, you can set aside time to use the prompt to write your own response before or after you read mine.

and/or

3. Find at least one other person and start your own group, using the guidelines on the next page and these prompts, the ones at the back, or ones you create yourself.

Whatever you decide, I hope you enjoy.

Andy Milberg

December 2021

Write to a Prompt Writers Group

Guidelines

(BRIEF INTRODUCTION AND ICE BREAKER IF NEW PEOPLE PRESENT)

1. After I finish giving you these guidelines, I will give a prompt to stimulate your creative juice, but you are invited to write on whatever you wish. If you can, let the words flow through you and out. Relax into it and have fun. We will write for 45 minutes. I will tell you when 40 minutes are up and 5 minutes remain so you can wrap it up.

2. When we finish writing, each will have an opportunity to read what they wrote and others may comment. It's your choice to read what you've written or not. No pressure. I'll say more about that when we are finished writing.

(READ THESE AFTER FINISHED WRITING AND BEFORE READING BEGINS.)

3. After each reading there will be a time to give comment on what was read. When commenting please tell what you liked or caught your attention. This is not meant to be a time to be a critic or make suggestion about how it could be better.

4. When commenting, in the interest of time, please stick to comments on what was read and avoid bringing in your own stories or similar experiences or going off on another subject. If someone expresses a problem or fear or being troubled, keep in mind that we are here to

listen, but not to fix.

5. Treat all that is read is fiction, but in case it's not, please keep what is expressed here as confidential and don't share what someone else has read with others who are not here.

Michael Koch

CONTENTS

CATCH

Prompt: CATCH

The field was overgrown with weeds and human waste. I could barely see the remnants of the base paths. Occasionally, the sound of a distant bird or gunshot pierced the silence.

Walking toward the slightly raised circle of grass and food wrappers that used to be the pitcher's mound, I felt the weight of what was lost. This forlorn place represented the accumulation of my life's cliche's…loss of youth, innocence, camaraderie, vitality, and hope.

Hey !

The sound of a human voice startled me, and I was immediately on alert.

Hey !

I turned to see a man standing behind where home plate would have been. He didn't seem threatening, but these days it was hard to know who to trust.

Wanna play catch ? He said, holding up what looked like an ancient, misshapen softball.

Sure, why not.

He threw the ball to me, and I almost caught it. Bending down to pick it up, the flash of back pain reminded me that I was not the healthy young boy who had been able to play for hours at a time so long ago.

C'mon. Throw it back, he said eagerly.

It had been decades since I threw anything other than a grenade.

As I began drawing back my arm, suddenly the years fell away.

Here it comes, I shouted, propelling the ball toward the eagerly awaiting hands of my new acquaintance. He caught it easily, and with what sounded like a laugh, threw it back immediately.

This time the ball met my hand and I felt a sense of joy that had been missing for a long time.

Nice catch, he shouted.

Thanks, I responded, and sent the ball back to him.

As the ball continued to fly back and forth, life became simpler. There was only me, the field, the man, and the ball.

Finally, he didn't throw it back. I waited. He looked at me, looked around, said "I have to go now.".

Wait, I said.

Thank you, I said.

He shrugged, and turned and walked away.

WHERE THE HELL ARE WE?

Prompt: Where the hell are we?

Joining hands and hearts, we began the journey. Our surroundings were a beautiful reflection of our state of being gentle sunlight, a cool breeze, the colors of the plants and flowers and trees, and the happy sounds of birds.

Perfect, you might think, and you would be right.

Neither of us had expected this when we met decades ago. Our separate paths had crossed a few times, with pleasant exchanges before we wandered away to other adventures.

Circumstances, or perhaps fate, had brought us together in a new way. We surrendered, and here we were. Here. Now. Co-creating a deeper and richer union than either of us had ever experienced. And now we were ready to take it to another level.

The molecules we had ingested began their gradual transformation of our consciousness. I became aware of a subtle shift, a change in my body, a kind of tingling as well as a lightening around my head. I realized my senses were heightening as I blinked and looked around, seeing my surroundings as if for the first time. Perhaps I was.

She sat quietly in front of me, a magnificent being emanating presence. Her green eyes invited me to connect wordlessly. My tendency to gush verbally dissolved as I released another layer of personality. She smiled in acknowledgment and appreciation. My heart filled with love and quickly radiated out through the confines of my body, first to her, then the room surrounding us, and continuing out through the walls, roof, sky, ever further, limitless, ever expanding.

Where the hell are we ? My mind tried to assert its need for reassurance, then realized it was irrelevant in that moment and relaxed. What a relief.

I reached for her hands at the same moment she reached for mine. Our skin seemed to merge. Beyond the physical connection, I felt the eternal energies of our Being surround and fill us, the beautiful chord of our separate notes being played together, the cosmic dance of Us.

Time stopped, or so it seemed. A burst of laughter at the sheer joy of the moment emerged, a familiar way for me to release energy that was getting too much for me to handle. She frowned.

There's more, she said, Go deeper.

For a moment I resisted, confused. She waited patiently, presently, inviting me to explore the unfamiliar with her.

I felt the tension in my body and the attempt at control in my mind. Then I remembered a line from The Hitchhiker's Guide to the Galaxy. Resistance is futile. I almost laughed again, and realized that truth. Resistance is futile.

I'm scared, I said.

She gently squeezed my hand and seemed to look deeper into my eyes, past my personna, my attachment to the personality I had worked so hard to create and maintain. I wanted to close my eyes and go into the place inside where I felt safe….and alone. I didn't.

I see you and I love you, she said.

As my tears began to flow, I felt a new peace envelop me and dissolve the dark areas inside that had always kept me separate from others, from her.

She knew.

Nice to be with you, she said.

STARING AT A BLANK CANVAS

Prompt: staring at a blank canvas

I turned around, compelled to look back one last time at the life I had led for the past 42 years, a life I was now leaving forever. As if I were dying, scenes from the past flashed through my mind at the speed of consciousness, so quickly I could not hold on to any, even if I wanted to.

There were some I cherished, some I regretted, a multitude of moments in time that were now irrelevant.

I noticed I was not breathing, and exhaled with a gasp.

Time to move on. Time. What a mystery.

Releasing the past, I turned my attention forward, took a step, and stopped.

I didn't have a clue what was next, and felt a combination of excitement and terror. A series of "what about's" churned through my mind as I stared at the blank canvas that was my future.

What's so was clear.

I am a relatively healthy human with no family, home, or job, accountable to no one. I have enough financial resources to have a multitude of choices about where to be and what to do. I have nothing to prove anymore.

The only question I need to answer is, what do I do with the rest of my life ?

****

I had that dream again, doctor.

The one where you leave everything behind and start over ?

Yes.

Was anything about it different this time ?

Not really.

So in the dream you completely forgot you had a wife, kids, house, job and dog ?

Yes.

And how did that feel ?

I don't know. Normal, liberating.

Say more about liberating.

Well, I was alone, and it was kind of ok. I think I liked the feeling of not having any responsibilities, of not having to deal with anybody or anything.

How have things been at home ?

Good, I guess. Of course, Sarah's been away visiting her mother for a week and the kids come and go as they please. And it's the slow season at work, so there hasn't been much for me to do there and none of us have to go to the office.

What do you do with your time ?

Walk the dog, surf the internet, watch tv, I don't know.

You don't sound very inspired.

I guess not.

OK. Let's try something. Imagine that you're staring at a blank canvas, that is your life. You can put anything you want on it, any experiences, any material stuff, any people. What comes to mind ?

I closed my eyes and tried to imagine what he was asking me to do.

****

When I opened them, I was in a beautiful house in Ajijic, Mexico. My wife was sitting at her desk, our little dog sleeping peacefully at her feet. She smiled at me and went back to her work. I walked outside. The gardens were colorful and lush, pleasing my eyes. The birds were singing, and the babies that had hatched in the past week were craning their little beaks out of the nests, waiting to be fed. The temperature was perfect and the sky was a clear blue, punctuated by a few wispy clouds that floated by. Mt. Garcia rose across the lake. I took a deep breath of clean, crisp air. Maybe I'll take a swim or soak in the hot tub. Maybe I'll play some music, or write something. Maybe I'll read. Maybe I'll take a walk to the village.

This is it, I thought. This is what I want.

FIRST CRIME

Prompt: First crime

No !

She looked at him, surprise in her eyes.

No ! He again exclaimed, shaking his head. It was time to go, yet he stood firm.

Why ? He asked. I don't understand, he said. It's not right, not fair.

She didn't answer. The tension grew with each frozen, eternal moment.

A distant sound broke the silence, startling them for a moment.

He looked at her, sadly or perhaps angrily, or perhaps neither. It was difficult to tell.

She sighed and ever so gently moved next to him, reaching for his hand. He didn't accept or resist her contact.

He turned and looked directly at her. There was nothing in his eyes that she could interpret.

The distant sound repeated.

Let's go, Adam.

She put her other hand on his back to guide him. He seemed to turn to stone for a moment, then surrendered and gave up. They started walking.

The bright sunlight and cool breeze enveloped them. Soft bird songs serenaded them as they walked through the lush landscape. The air was fragrant.

Tears streamed down her eyes, while his remained fixed and empty. The path grew rougher as they approached the boundaries of what had been their home.

God's trumpet sounded again.

Time to leave the garden.

SHOULD I BE WORRIED?

PROMPT: Should I be worried ?

The dream lingered at the edge of my conscious awareness, teasing me with wisps of images that danced away as I reached for them. My efforts to remember details were useless, so I tried to recall a general sense of where I was, who else was there, anything to re-create the sensations, feelings and thoughts that had captivated me before I awoke abruptly.

For some reason it felt important.

I closed my eyes and relaxed my body. Nothing.

Feeling frustrated, I opened them again, planning to begin transitioning into my morning routine. Something seemed different. I looked over at my wife, sleeping with her back to me. She seemed what was it ? I wasn't sure.

I got out of bed and walked to the kitchen. The dog followed me, as usual. My father was already there, waiting.

Good morning, he said, did you sleep well ?

Fine, I answered, and then remembered that he had been dead for two years.

What's going on ?, I thought.

He smiled.

The dog barked, wanting to go out.

I walked to the door to let him out. It was still dark, unusual for this time of day. Or was it day ? Maybe I was still dreaming.

When the dogs returned, the three of us returned to bed. I looked over to where my wife used to sleep and felt the hurt that was only now beginning to fade since she left me.

Everything will feel better in the morning, I thought, or maybe not. Should I be worried ? There was certainly enough to worry about, aside from my lonely life. Fires surrounded me, covid was renewing its relentless toll on humanity, the government was turning more authoritarian by the hour, and my hair was falling out.

I woke up to rain, lightning, and thunder. Going out to the porch, I sat and watched nature's nightly show, marveling at its majesty. It would have been nice to have someone to share it with, even a dog or two, but I was alone. Its ok, I told myself. I watched a little while longer, wiped the tears from my eyes, and went back to bed.

Maybe I fell back asleep, maybe not. It might have been minutes, or hours later when a familiar voice pierced my consciousness.

Time to get up, honey ! The driver picks us up in an hour and we don't want to be late for our flight. I'm so excited that we're finally moving to Mexico.

What flight ? There haven't been any flights for months. And moving to Mexico ?

I gave up trying to figure it all out and went back to sleep.

WHAT DOES IT MEAN?

Prompt: What does it mean ?

Everything looks the same and feels......totally different, new, and....strange.

I'm the same, or think I am, but maybe I'm wrong.

What am I certain of ?

It is the year 2021, I have a male body, which is in a small village in Mexico on the shore of the largest lake in Mexico.

I am 73 years old. Wait.....there's something about that that doesn't feel real. What does it mean ? I know it's a number representing the years I've been alive, but I have a hard time relating to it. Do I feel 73 ? I'm not sure what 73 is supposed to feel like.

I could go around and around in my head about this for a long time.

Time. What does it mean ?

So I look around again. Yes, this is where I live, in this beautiful house, and the woman standing in front of me is my beautiful wife, and she is smiling at me and welcoming me home, and I'm observing myself hugging her and feeling......I don't know. Disoriented. Surreal. Confused.

Our dog died recently, after sharing life with us for 8 ½ years. I'm not sure how long ago because something happened inside me and I needed rest (they said) and full time care (they said) and medication (they said).

And then they said I was ready to go home, and here I am.

Home. What does it mean ?

Home used to be the place where I lived with my wife and dog, the three of us a family, energetically interconnected and sharing our lives fully. I avoided thinking about a future where one of us was no longer there, denying the inevitable.

And now that is the reality.

Reality ? What does it mean ?

I suppose it means starting a new life together with my wife, without the constant presence of that little four legged being we both loved so much. It means re-discovering who we are as a couple. It means accepting the inevitable changes that occur that we have no control over. It means recognizing the reality and permanence of death so that we can live more fully while we are alive, knowing that we don't and can't know how long we have left.

And it means accepting that there will likely be moments of grief for the loss, and that's ok.

I look around. I'm alive. I love living here, in this home, in this village, and I love my wife. And that means everything.

I AM MOST HAPPY WHEN....

Prompt: I am most happy when _____

She gave me what I interpreted as an all too familiar look. I braced myself for what I was about to hear.

"Thank you for taking care of that. It's exactly what I wanted. I really appreciate it."

What ? I thought. I wasn't expecting that.

"In fact, I want to show you how much I appreciate it", she said, taking my hand and leading me into the bedroom.

A few hours later, I looked into her eyes and said, "Wow".

She smiled and purred back at me, snuggling closer.

Life is good, I thought.

Reflecting on the afternoon's events, I realized that I am most happy when I am engaged in a creative project, when I am doing things for my Beloved and lovemaking with my Beloved. And today included all of them. What a blessing.

Of course, I couldn't just leave it there. I had to go deeper into this inquiry into the nature of happiness. And that's when the intellectual mental masturbation began, filling up time I could have put to more enjoyable and satisfying use.

Should my happiness depend on anything external to me ? Doesn't that put me at the effect of other people and circumstances?

Is my essential nature happy, or is that a mental concept ? Is happiness an illusion in the midst of universal human suffering?

What is happiness, anyway? Would everyone agree on the same definition? If not, then is happiness so subjective as to be meaningless?

What would someone from another culture say is happiness ?

When do I know I'm happy ? What does happiness feel like ?

Blah, blah, blah.

"Where are you ?", she asked, knowing me so well.

I looked at her and chuckled.

"Sorry. Got lost in my head again."

"I noticed", she said with a smile. Her eyes began to transmit an invitation.

"Wouldn't you rather be here with me ?" she said in that sultry voice I loved to hear.

She reached down with her hand. My body reminded me that it was available for more fun than my mind provided.

An hour later, she dozed in my arms and I began to start thinking about happiness again.

"Not yet", my body said, basking in the afterglow. And as the currents of pleasure began to subside, I relaxed into true happiness.

DID YOU BRING IT?

Prompt: Did you bring it ?

I settled into the chair, reached for the water glass, and drained it.

More ?, he asked, and then got up to refill the glass when I nodded.

He sat down and looked at me, patiently.

Where to start ? I thought, fidgeting slightly.

His eyes held mine with a clear message…..no rush.

Taking a deep breath, I said "this week has been better."

"Tell me more about that" I heard him say in my mind.

"I've been trying to follow the Physician's Oath…first do no harm. So I'm really paying attention to when I feel triggered, and monitoring what I say and the tone of my voice. It still feels like I'm navigating a minefield and things could blow up a lot of the time, especially when we get into a conversation, but there have also been more moments of peace and connection."

"How are you showing up that creates that peace and connection ? he asked.

Shit, I thought. I'd rather talk about how she is and what she does to create the minefield.

"Well, I think I'm listening to her in a deeper way, and recognizing when I start to make up a story about what she's saying. So I'm not as reactive.

And that's helping me stay connected more to my heart, which is important because it reminds me how much I love her."

That sounds good, he said.

But, I thought.

Is there something else ? he asked.

Damn, he's good, I thought, but I'm not going to talk about that yet.

"Well, there's still the dog thing. It's only been two months since Buffy died. Diane's ready for a new one, I'm don't think I am. She spends hours every day online looking, and has actually filled out adoption papers for a few. Some of them look really cute, and I have to admit that I miss dog energy in the house, but I want to go on the road trip we've been talking about and don't want to either take a dog or think about a dog while we're traveling. I just want to enjoy the trip."

"That sounds reasonable to me. Have you told her ?"

"Yes, and she agrees, but I sometimes want to go out and get another dog or two immediately."

I stopped talking and took a long gulp of water.

He knew.

"What are you avoiding talking about ?" he asked gently.

I drained the glass quickly. He refilled it and looked at me.

I looked up at the clock. Too much time left. I looked out the window. My throat felt dry.

"I feel like I don't know how I'm supposed to live at this stage of my life or how I want to. Who the fuck am I ? So many of the identities I've held about myself in the past are obsolete, due to changes and aging. I'm confused and probably scared that my life is getting smaller and limited. Death doesn't scare me, theoretically, but living with these feelings isn't exciting or joyful. What's the point of doing everything I'm doing to maintain my health and live longer ?

He nodded.

"Time's up, he said, same time next week ?"

I nodded.

Getting in my car, I made a decision.

She was working in the garden when I got home. When she saw me reach into the back seat, her eyes lit up.

Did you bring it ? she asked.

The puppy in my arms answered her question.

The answers to my other questions would have to wait.

SHIFT HAPPENS

Prompt: Shift happens

I awoke abruptly, disturbed by unsettling dream images, thought "this is no way to start the day", and closed my eyes.

What seemed like hours later, I opened them again. "Better" I thought, seeing the dog's furry face next to mine and my wife behind him. Making sure they were both breathing, I relaxed and contemplated the day ahead.

Another day in pandemic paradise.

Looking out the window at the lush garden and reflection of the sun on the lake, I again appreciated the natural beauty surrounding us. If I have to be stuck at home, this was the place to be.

Easing out of bed so I didn't disturb my family, I went to the bathroom, dressed, then walked to the kitchen to prepare breakfast. The morning sounds from the neighborhood permeated the house, birds, dogs, an occasional car, truck or motorcycle going by. I considered asking Alexa to play some music, then changed my mind.

After preparing breakfast, I took it to the office and turned on the computer. Emails and stock market checked, I switched to live news.

What ????? Is that really possible ?

Our beloved president was waving goodbye as he got on the helicopter, leaving his post to a usurper who had stolen the election, abandoning those of us who supported him through all the attacks on him during the past five years. How could he betray us like this ?

The illegal incoming regime was supposed to be arrested so that our country would continue its mission of greatness, under his leadership. And yet they were being sworn in, with our patriots nowhere in sight.

How could this happen when the truth was obvious ? It must be that the dark forces of the deep state had taken over the media and made fake news seem real, as well as brainwashing the politicians to go along with this charade.

It was time. I never thought it would come to this, but I opened the desk drawer and took out the button, the red button I had never expected to need. Taking a deep breath, I steeled my resolve. My hand began to move toward it, my finger extending to take this irrevocable action that would impact the world in ways I might never live to see.

As I pressed down, I could sense a trembling in the very fabric of being, a reverberation beginning to extend out into the universe, a shift happening to everything old as the new world order began to establish itself.

I awoke abruptly, disturbed by unsettling dream images, and looked at the dog's furry face on the pillow next to me and my wife behind him. Making sure they were both breathing, I relaxed and contemplated the day ahead.

PLEASE TAKE A NUMBER

Prompt: Please take a number

Humans are annoying. Since coming to this planet, I have increasingly observed this, especially in english speaking countries during the past 5 years. Perhaps annoying is not the most accurate word for them, but I'm trying to be kind.

Enough of that. Humans are irrational, overemotional, selfish, ignorant, uncooperative, deplorable, frustrating, infuriating, and mostly disgusting creatures. To be fair, I will admit, however, that I've met a few who maintained the appearance of being kind and loving, at least until they felt slighted or threatened.

So what am I doing here ? It started when the intergalactic multi dimensional council called a meeting, and we all tuned in from wherever we happened to be in space or time. Cosmic warning signals had put this planet on the agenda. It was decided that it was prudent to take a closer look at what was happening here, especially since humans first discovered the means to kill masses of their fellow species with a single explosion, and then began to venture outside their own atmosphere.

Although they were still extremely far away from being able to affect (and infect) other life forms, there was agreement that there was no reason to take any chances of them polluting innocents.

So we all took a number between zero and infinity, and mine was called. I shudder, remembering that moment. What were the odds ?

All I wanted was to live out my remaining millenia drifting formlessly through the quiet vastness, occasionally taking on the shape of whatever material life forms I encountered and enjoying a temporary experience of corporality.

Now I was stuck on this physically beautiful, but increasingly rotting ball of conflict and chaos called earth, babysitting a race that seemed committed to finding some way of destroying itself, which from my perspective wouldn't be a bad thing.

None of them knew of my existence, although the more expansive minded (who were labeled as crazy and/or conspiracy theorists) created detailed stories about my presence. It was amusing to hear their description of us. Lizards ? Grays ? Ha ! The truth is so beyond their puny minds' ability to grasp.

So I live among them, watching, recording everything, sending the data back to my colleagues, hoping without much hope that the perceived threat will be reduced and I will once again be able to release form and leave. Meanwhile, I enjoy what is available in this little Mexican lakeside village, participating in the human activities without arousing suspicion of my true nature.

I DON'T BELONG HERE

Prompt: I don't belong here

We seemed to be having a good time, when suddenly she pulled away.

What's the matter ? I asked, trying to catch my breath.

I don't belong here, she said, clutching the sheet to her chest.

I've got to get out of here. Now.

She threw off the sheet, left the bed, and began to gather her clothes.

Wait, Angela, I implored. Let's talk about this. I don't understand.

She ignored my request and continued dressing.

Was it something I said or did ?

No. Not everything is about you.

Without looking back, she left the room, and I heard the front door close.

That was weird, I thought. Now what ?

I went into the bathroom to pee, considering my next move. It was still early. Do I want to go to sleep ? No. Watch something on Netflix ? No. Maybe I should go back to the club. Why not ?

I took a quick shower and dressed, thinking about what had happened. She had seemed nice and I was immediately attracted to her when we began talking earlier. She seemed interested in me, too. After our second drink, I asked if she wanted to go someplace quieter, like my apartment, and she eagerly accepted.

When we got inside the front door, I turned to face her and she immediately put her arms around me and gave me a passionate kiss, which continued as we moved to the bedroom. Clothes came off and all seemed to be well until she stopped abruptly.

OK. Another story to remember, or not. Time to move on.

I dressed and headed out, on to the next adventure.

The club was still crowded when I entered. I walked to the bar, caught the bartender's eye and ordered a margarita. Turning around, I surveyed the scene, looking for possibilities to salvage the evening.

She caught my eye and smiled.

I walked over to where she was standing.

Hi. My name's Michael.

Angela. Nice to meet you.

We chatted about this or that while we finished our drinks.

Another ? I asked.

Sure. Thank you.

As we completed the next round, I asked if she wanted to leave, and received an enthusiastic "Yes".

When we got inside the front door, I turned to face her and she immediately put her arms around me and gave me a passionate kiss, which continued as we moved to the bedroom. Clothes came off and all seemed to be going well until she stopped abruptly.

What's the matter ? I asked, trying to catch my breath.

I don't belong here, she said, clutching the sheet to her chest.

I've got to get out of here. Now.

DRUM BEATS IN
THE NIGHT

Prompt: DRUM BEATS IN THE NIGHT

The van rolled through the countryside, engine purring as if it enjoyed traveling through the dense forests surrounding us as much as we did. Canada in early August was a myriad of green, many shades shifting rapidly as we headed north, my traveling partner humming happily next to me.

This was our first road trip, a celebration of two years together, and the maiden journey of our new old camper van. So far there were no breakdowns mechanically or emotionally.

Starting in Palo Alto, California, we meandered up the coast at a leisurely pace, enjoying the scenery and each other. The surroundings shifted from redwoods and sand dunes to forests and mountain peaks, delighting all our senses.

Our destination was an annual Native American pow wow in British Columbia, a few hours north of Vancouver. We planned to arrive in early afternoon and set up camp. Miscalculating the driving time, we rolled in after dark, tired, hungry and a bit cranky.

A friendly face greeted us at the gate.

"Welcome."

I responded with as much of a grin as I could muster.

"Thanks. We'd like a campsite, please."

She frowned, and said, "There are only a few spaces left. I have to warn you that they are very close to where the drumming circle will

46

be playing all night."

I looked at my companion. Something passed between us wordlessly and we both said at the same time….

"YES !"

Our host seemed surprised. "OK, then".

We paid, received directions to the site, and began to drive.

The sound began as a deep throb, pulsating through the darkness as we approached. An orange glow grew brighter in the moonless night, as the drum beats grew louder. We felt the rhythm resonating in our bodies as we parked, energy building.

As soon as we were settled, we were out the doors and headed closer. It was hard to tell how many drummers were there, and we didn't care. Fatigue and hunger disappeared. Every cell in our bodies responded to the primal call of movement and motion. We danced wildly, sometime together, sometimes apart, mostly oblivious to irrelevant identities we paraded around in day to day life.

Who knows how long later, we returned to our camp site.

Who know how long later, our bodies separated and we fell into a deeply satiated sleep.

ANOTHER MISSED OPPORTUNITY

Prompt: Another missed opportunity

I was pretty stoned when she whispered in my ear, her words mingling with Pink Floyd's Dark Side of the Moon blaring from the speakers. So I simply nodded and continued trying to fathom the lyrics that seemed like the most profound thing I had ever heard.

She snuggled closer to me. I liked that for a moment, then the music built to another crescendo of guitars and drums creating a resonant vibration in every cell of my being, connecting me with the eternal Om of the universe. I closed my eyes and surrendered to the cosmic sounds, dissolving into oneness. Life is good.

Decades later, she was no longer there. Neither was the room I remembered. Or my twenty year old self.

Instead, I was just a somewhat normal person playing out a predictable routine. Wake to the alarm, get out of bed, shower, shave, coffee and a muffin, out the door to the office for eight soul numbing hours analyzing numbers, then to the bar for a few drinks before picking up a fast food dinner, gobbling it down, finally going home to eventually fall asleep with the tv playing the latest trendy series.

Some would say I was lucky to have a lucrative job in the current economy, a roof over my head, good health.

What opportunities am I missing? What opportunities have I missed?

I didn't think much about that, thanks to the meds. After my divorce and suicide attempt, it had taken, I'm not sure, a year or two, maybe five, to find the right combination of molecules to regulate my brain chemistry. Now I was considered stable enough to live on my own and support myself.

Maybe I should get a dog? But I'd have to leave him home alone all day and he probably wouldn't like that.

I signed up on a dating site a few years ago, but that didn't go well. Maybe I wasn't ready. Maybe I am now. Maybe not.

My life is good. I have a nice apartment and a well paying job. Am I missing something?

What shall I watch tonight?

RAIN CHECK

Prompt: RAIN CHECK

The combination of sunshine, a cool breeze, the softness of the meadow grass, and her beauty was intoxicating. I thought, briefly, that I was the luckiest sixteen year old on the planet. That thought, and all others, quickly evaporated as our lips met.

She had moved into town last year, making an immediate impression on all the high school boys. Each made an attempt to make her feel comfortable, trying not to be obvious about their similar agenda. The local girls, sensing a threat, were more overt in protecting their interests. She was not invited to their parties.

I watched this adolescent social dance play out, sometimes amused, sometimes appalled. My focus was on my studies, my ticket out of this small town life. My classmates went to sporting events and got wasted on the weekends. I went to the library to study, away from the chaos and conflict at home.

She was often there, for her own unknown reasons. We would nod to each other in passing, nothing more. Until today.

So here we were, two teenagers discovering and exploring new realms of pleasure. Uncontrollable hormones flooded our bodies along with the terror of not knowing where this would lead us or how to get there.

Our lips felt good together. My hands began to explore, both tentatively and urgently. She met me with what felt like that same combination of desire and fear.

The sun was suddenly blocked by rapidly moving clouds, and the temperature began to drop. Thunder signaled an approaching storm.

And we paused, losing the moment that would have changed our lives in ways we could not know.

"I have to get home", she said, averting her eyes.

"Me, too", I replied.

STOP FOR A MOMENT, THINK ABOUT WHAT JUST HAPPENED

Prompt: Stop for a moment; think about what just happened.

Stop for a moment. Think about what just happened., she said.

I don't want to. Leave me alone., I thought.

OK., I said.

So ? She said.

So what ? I thought.

I guess I was wrong., I said. I'm sorry.

OK,. She said, and I thought I was off the hook, until she said, "so why did you do it ?"

Because I wanted to, I thought.

Because I wasn't thinking, I said.

Will you think about it next time ? She asked.

Of course, I said.

Maybe, I thought.

Give me a break, I thought.

Thank you, I'd really appreciate that., she said.

Can I go back to watching the game now ? I thought.

OK, I said, you know I never want to do anything that hurts you.

I know, she said, just pay more attention to what you're doing.

Yes, Mom, I thought.

I'll try to do better, I said.

Don't try, she said,. Just do it.

Now I have to listen to a fucking Nike commercial, I thought.

OK, I will, I said.

Can I remind you ? She said.

Can I stop you ?, I thought.

Of course, I said. I'll appreciate that.

Are you sure ?, she said.

Definitely not, I thought.

I said yes, I said, defensively.

Don't get defensive, she said, I'm only trying to help.

I appreciate that, I said.

I resent that, I thought.

I'm not your enemy, she said.

I know, I said.

Sometimes you are, I thought.

Sometimes you forget that, she said.

I know, I said., I'm sorry.

Can I go now? I thought.

This doesn't feel good, she said, Stop for a moment. Think about what just happened.

FAIR IS FAIR

Prompt: Fair is fair

They say fair is fair, and that may be true, except when it isn't.

Silence was the difference as I walked into the room for the last time. A week of constant sounds coming from machines prolonging her life was suddenly over, the quiet representing clear evidence of their failure.

Her body lay unencumbered by the tubes that had defined her final identity, a patient struggling to survive literal heartbreak. Now she was, what?

I sat and took her hand, remembering.

We had met almost thirty years earlier at a bookstore in San Francisco. She had just returned from a volunteer mission in Nicaragua. I was struck immediately by her beauty and the sparkle in her eyes, along with her dedication and passion for making the world a better place.

Within months we were living together, soon to marry, eventually to separate before she birthed our child. When he was nine, she had her first heart attack, which only temporarily paused her constant quest for justice and a healthy planet.

A little over ten years later, after making healthier personal lifestyle choices and continuing the work she had dedicated her life to, it was time to retire and relax into enjoying things she loved but had put aside in her relentless commitment.

It was a beautiful fall morning and she decided to go for a hike. As she dressed, she noticed a pain in her arm, which as usual she tried to minimize. When it increased, she decided to go to the doctor. As she was being examined, she suffered a massive heart attack.

A week in intensive care had led to this moment.

A mixture of feelings flooded me, primarily the unfairness. She was a person who had dedicated, some would say sacrificed, most of her life for a larger vision, delaying her own pursuits of pleasure. And now, when she could have begun to slow down and enjoy the fruits of her labor, this.

Along with sadness, I was filled with anger. This wasn't right. She deserved better. Fair is fair? Bullshit !

In the years since her dying, I continue to try to make sense of life, death, and the human condition, especially as I and my friends age, get sick, and also die. Despair is always lurking at the edge of my consciousness, waiting to envelop me and drag me down to a place where nothing matters and I don't matter.

Fortunately, some stronger force holds me, an energy that gently yet powerfully lets me know that there is a bigger picture that I will never understand no matter how much I try to figure it out. It tells me that although life may not seem fair, or even be fair, it is still Life with a capital L, holding all there is, including me.

And for some irrational reason that gives me comfort, even if temporary.

LOVE OF MY LIFE

Prompt: Love of my life

Fred turned his head at the sound of his name being called. The voice was vaguely familiar.

"Fred, that's you, isn't it ?", she said again, walking toward him. Her face showed a mixture of pleasant surprise and caution.

He looked at her, and fuzzy memories began to bubble up from forgotten places in his long history.

"Hello", he said tentatively.

She stopped.

"Don't you remember me?" she asked.

He sighed.

"I'm not sure. I think so. But not details. I'm sorry."

She took a deep breath.

"I'm Sara."

"Sara" Obsolete circuits within his brain sparked. "Sara ! We went out when we were in college together, didn't we ?".

Sara carefully considered what to say next.

"Yes, but I would say it was more than just going out, Fred. We were together three years. And talked about getting married."

Fred felt a throb in the back of his head, and a familiar confusion enveloped him. What should he say now ?

66

"Well, Sara. How have you been ?"

He immediately felt stupid.

"How have I been ? You haven't seen me in some fifty years, and after what happened between us, you ask how I have been ? What's wrong with you ?"

A wave of what might have been shame washed over Fred, then retreated quickly, as all of his emotions seemed to.

He stammered, "I'm sorry. Since Vietnam I've had a really hard time relating to people, and my meds affect my memory."

She softened, and tears began to flow down her face.

"I'm sorry, too, Fred. It's just that you completely disappeared and here you are, reminding me of all that we shared and all that we talked about. You were and are the love of my life. I've never forgotten you."

Fred heard her words, and tried to feel something. Love of her life ? What did that mean? And why did she tell him that now ? What did she want from him ?

"Say something, Fred", she implored.

What could he say ? He looked at her, and began to robotically repeat a story he had told so many times before.

"I don't remember much from those years. I think I went straight into a hospital when I came back, and didn't want anyone I knew to see me like that. The doctor I talked to encouraged me to have a fresh start and I thought he meant I should not contact anyone I knew. I moved

67

out west and have been drifting around for a long time."

"So you haven't married or had a family?"

"No."

"Me, neither."

Fred looked at her, then looked around. He looked back at her and realized that she was a stranger talking to him about something. What was it ? He waited, ready to run or attack or do whatever he had to.

The expression in her eyes, changed, hardened.

"Well, I need to get going. It was nice, no, it was interesting seeing you."

Fred's body relaxed.

"OK", he said

She turned and walked away.

ROSES AND A SMILE

PROMPT: Roses and a smile

A flash of red among the empty wine bottles and soggy take out cartons caught my eye. Looking closer, I was surprised to see a bouquet of roses. Carefully removing the trash that partially covered it, I surveyed my new treasure. Aside from a small smear of what looked like soy sauce, they appeared pristine. I lifted them up to examine more closely. There were eleven, held together by a white ribbon. No card.

I climbed out of the dumpster, clutching the partially rotten and eaten fruits and vegetables, and the flowers. The food went into my backpack, reducing the chances I would be robbed on the way back to the bridge.

Listening to the shouts coming from around the corner, I realized it was time to move quickly, before getting caught in the middle of the morning confrontation. Getting back to our relatively safe haven was more challenging as the weeks went on, but I had to venture out if we wanted to eat.

I headed west, toward the river, staying close to the boarded up buildings, then through an alley I was familiar with. I didn't know if the bodies I passed were dead or alive, and I didn't stop to find out. There had been a time when I would have cared. No more.

As I approached the end of the alley, the sound of automatic weapons made me pause. I peeked around the corner and saw several khaki clad figures firing at a storefront across the street. After a few minutes, they stopped and stormed the building.

This was my chance. I ran down the street toward the bridge, bracing for the bullet that I had been dodging since the New Order had begun, praying that I would get to see my family again. Each step brought me closer to the only reason I had to live in these trying times.

"STOP !" I heard from behind me. I didn't, plunging into the rubble that separated the streets from the river. Here I was relatively safe. I slowed down and gasped for air, feeling a relief I could never again take for granted.

The bridge took another ten minutes to reach. And there they were, watching me approach with their eyes reflecting the worry and fear that was our constant reminder of what life had become.

I handed her the bouquet of roses.

She smiled, and burst into tears.

A CASE OF
CORRUPTION

PROMPT: A case of corruption

The warehouse is mostly full, boss. I don't know what we're going to do with a lot of the old merchandise. Since Biden was elected we're not moving the stuff nearly as fast as we did with trump. We need to light a fire under the sales team, they're getting lazy. Or maybe they don't want to work anymore since they're getting all this stimulus money. I've got cases of nepotism rotting in the back room, federal judge appointments drinking kool aid in the corner, and business bribery cases trying to bribe each other.

And there's a huge case of corruption sitting on the dock with no place to store it. It was ordered last summer, before the election, but the factory was so back-ordered at that time it took awhile to fill. Maybe DeSantis would be willing to take it off our hands if we give him a deal.

If all else fails, we can unload it to some third world country at a decent price.

The good news is that we got rid of all the inventory of sex scandal. There's always some conservative who needs a few of those, and Gaetz bought all the remaining stock. And cases of lies and gaslighting are flying out the door. Cruz just placed another big order. As long as we have a republican party and fox news, we'll never have a problem moving those, let's order some more, for immediate delivery.

Can we consider ordering some science again ? It used to be a good seller until 5 years ago, and might be coming back into fashion, at least with half the population.

Social justice and equality also seem to be making a comeback, especially with the younger generation. I could order a few cases and see how they move during the next few years, but wouldn't want to over order and get stuck with them. You know how fickle our clientele is.

In general, it's business as usual.

So the last thing I wanted to talk to you about is, can I get a raise ?

SHE CLIMBED ABOARD THE MIDNIGHT BUS

Prompt: She climbed aboard the midnight bus and collapsed in a seat next to a man who appeared to be absorbed in his thoughts.

So tired. Started at 8 in the morning, expecting to go home at 5, and now it was almost midnight. Please let the bus be on time.

The day had seemed normal, treating the usual number of patients in the emergency room with their variety of injuries and ailments. At least until the ambulances began to arrive in mid-afternoon. Another fired employee returning to his former workplace, his frustration and fear having built to murderous desperation as the unpaid bills piled up.

We didn't know any of this. All we knew were the bleeding bodies that required all our skills to survive. And so we worked without a break, assessing, stabilizing, stitching, and sending those we couldn't save to the morgue.

And finally I could go home to my husband, to rest and try to forget the suffering I had witnessed this day.

The bus was late.

I sighed and scrolled through the newsfeed on my phone. More details on the shooting, interviews with survivors and weeping family members, and a vague description of the shooter, who had reportedly been shot by the first police responders before he escaped the scene.

The hiss of brakes signaled the arrival of the bus. I got on, expecting it to be empty, and was surprised to see only a few empty seats. Then I remembered that during the cold months, the ever increasing homeless would ride the night buses as long as possible to stay warm.

I took one of the few available seats near the front, feeling the relief of finally being off my feet. The man in the seat next to me seemed to be lost in thought, his head down and his hat covering his face. Good. I was in no mood for conversation.

I hoped that Paul would be asleep when I got home. Although I loved his attention and that he was always interested in how my day went, today was an exception. Sounds of screams and tears, and images of blood and gore would need to fade before I felt like relating to him or anyone.

My seatmate stirred and seemed to groan. I did my best to ignore him. He murmured something I didn't understand.

Thankfully, my stop was approaching. In another 10 minutes I would be home, closing my front door and leaving behind the events of the day and the pain of a world that seemed to be growing more and more dangerous.

I reached up to pull the cord signaling the driver to stop, then began to stand and move toward the door.

The man next to me looked up. Our eyes met. He seemed to be silently pleading.

I turned away quickly and made my exit. The darkness and silence of the night embraced me as I walked down the block to my home. I closed the door, took a deep breath, and my tears began to flow.

JUST JUMP OVER THE WALL

Prompt: Just jump over the wall

Change is coming.

No, it's here.

The dialogue inside Fred's head began as soon as he opened his eyes. Are you sure ?

Haven't you been reading the news for the past year and a half ? Or seen faces hidden behind masks every time you used to go out ?

Fred closed his eyes again, hoping for some silence. No such luck.

When are we going back to normal ?

You think we're ever going back to normal ? Ha ! Wake up.

Fred's eyes opened again. He looked around. Nothing seemed different. Dirty clothes were piled in the corner, dishes overflowing the sink. The computer screensaver glowed on the desk. No sounds came from the city streets. Is this the new normal ?, he thought.

Maybe. Or things could get worse.

Fred considered his options for the day. There was no office to go to, and no work to do online, now that the company was outsourcing.

Maybe I'll take a shower and shave. It's been a few days.

Why bother ?

Nevermind. I'm hungry.

Take your pill first.

OK. Now what can I eat that doesn't require cleaning a pot or plate ?

His opened the kitchen cabinet. Ah Protein bars.

Opening the wrapper and tossing it on the floor, he sat down at his desk and took a bite.

They used to taste better, didn't they ?

Get used to them. And be grateful you have something. A lot of people don't.

Fred sighed. I don't want to think about that.

He looked out the window at the windows of the building facing him.

Hmmm. Haven't seen anyone in awhile.

Continuing to chew without tasting, he turned his attention to the computer screen and the chess game he was playing with someone in some unidentified part of the world.

I think I'm going to win this game.

So what ?

Why are you always so negative ?

You know the answer to that.

After a few moves, he surrendered. A message flashed on the screen.....you are invited to play another game with Rodney442x. Fred declined.

What now ?

I don't know. Maybe a walk through the park ? Oh right, quarantine is still in place. I could call Rita. Oh right, she died last month.

Fred felt his mood lifting. The pill was taking effect.

What day is it ?

Thursday.

Isn't there something I do on Thursdays ?

Think, Fred.

That's it, the writing group ! What time is it ?

Fred opened his email account to see if the prompt had arrived yet. There it was......"just jump over the wall".

What a stupid prompt, he thought, and began writing.

Forty five minutes later, he stopped and read over what he had written.

That's great !, he thought, and listened for any rebuttal.

There was none. Life is good.

STEP THROUGH
THE DOOR

PROMPT: Step through the door

No way I'm stepping through that door ! That door leads to the unknown. And that's terrifying.

It's not so bad here. Most of the time. Some of the time. More mindfucking.

Go ahead. Step through the door.

I'm scared.

Step anyway.

I want to stay here. It's familiar.

You can't. Life doesn't work that way.

I regress into a scared little boy looking out at a world I don't understand, desperately trying to figure out the rules and where I fit. What I know is that I can't go back and I can't stay here.

Time. Time moves forward. Time to move.

I am frozen, paralyzed with self doubt. Will I survive ?

Time to take one step. Then another.

That wasn't so bad. I survived.

Another step.

The door disappears and I am somewhere new.

I survived. Now what ?

Now I am surrounded by possibilities, and a spark of curiosity emerges.

There's a writer's group I never knew about.

I forgot about how much I love playing music.

There's so much to learn about history.

My Spanish is ok, and I can improve.

My partner and I can have new adventures together.

My fear dissolves, replaced by inspiration, excitement and energy.

Challenges are no longer overwhelming or debilitating.

New doors are now visible that were always there, inviting.

More, and more, and more.

Keep moving.

No. I have to stop and rest.

Step through the door.

Too much pressure. I can't. I don't want to. Leave me alone.

And although the externals are different, I am back again at the crossroad of my life, struggling with time and change.

No way I'm stepping through that door !

Eventually, I always do.

THERE I WAS, SURROUNDED

Prompt: there I was, surrounded

It began as a normal day, waking to the sounds of neighborhood dogs creating yet another unique symphony. I listened for awhile to the cacophony of canine expressions. Some would have judged it as noise, but I didn't mind.

After my usual bathroom routine, I dressed, had breakfast, and turned on the computer to check my calendar, an old habit now obsolete, like so many others.

I sighed, reflected on how much my life had changed, and considered what trivial distraction I would turn my attention to today, filling the time until I went back to sleep.

The dogs silent, it was time for the nearby construction noise to begin, the pile drivers creating an almost hypnotic rhythm that would be the backbeat for the next few hours, until mid-day siesta time. What were they building over there, I thought, and for who ?

A walk to the lake ! That could kill an hour or two.

The air felt clear and crisp as I left the house, looking around to survey the street, which was empty as usual. It had been a long time since I had seen any neighbors.

It was now time to make a choice, turn left or right. I considered the pro's and con's of each, which were equal so it really didn't matter, did it ? The last time I ventured out I turned right. So should I go left this time ? After pondering this meaningless question for a few moments, I turned right and began to walk.

Passing the field around the corner, I stopped to count the cows, which were grazing whatever vegetation that remained. There were three less than I remembered. I counted again to make sure, then wondered what had happened to them, considering a variety of possibilities.

Time to move on. The path began to descend as I approached the lake, so I had to walk even slower, carefully paying attention to each step. Heel, toe, heel, toe, heel toe. When it became too much of an effort to keep track, I stopped to rest. Then I began again. Heel, toe, heel, toe.

Until I reached the edge of the lake, and looked around.

There I was, surrounded by natural beauty, filling me with an indescribable feeling that dissolved all thought. The water glistened in the sunshine, and gentle waves were lapping onto the shore with a comforting sound, bringing me present to this moment, and this, and this.

Until I thought, isn't there something I have to do today ?

RIVERS OF LIFE

RIVERS OF LIFE

Old white men hang on like dying dinosaurs

to a burning world. Ash chokes their desperate bleating,

and rivers of fire, wind, and water encompass their futile attempts

to maintain control of an obsolete (dis)order..

Desperate protests grow fainter as new voices emerge,

the sounds of young cyber heroes shaping creation.

Handmaidens continue to serve, fearful of changing roles,

as their carefully constructed castles crumble.

The fire burns their fantasies,

and soon they stand naked and trembling,

looking for new saviors to worship and obey.

What is to be if we let go of what we have known ?

The unknown invites hope and endless possibilities,

and many respond with fear of loss,

Unwilling or unable to surrender to the inevitable.

Biology trumps ideology.

Earth, out of balance from greed and pollution, seeks a more organic solution.

Humans be damned, and if not damned,

sick and dying at the hand of a microscopic enemy,

or crushed by an unsustainable economic philosophy

that rewards the few and spreads crumbs for most,

who struggle for survival and accept their fate,

distracted by the drama and fantasies that cloak their despair.

And it really doesn't matter, does it,

From the perspective of eternity ?

All that live age, die and decay,

decomposing into new forms, fertilizing the future.

Life will live on, at least until the sun burns out,

and the planet becomes a cinder speck floating in space.

Meanwhile, caught up in our quest for security and meaning,

We might as well lighten up and enjoy the ride.

RITUALS

Prompt: Rituals

The day begins with a pee, then a trip to the kitchen, gradually transitioning from my dream state to whatever passes for reality.

Two pieces of toast or three ? The first major decision of the day. Usually two. Today is two.

Avocado or not. Second decision. Usually yes. Today, no.

I take a plate and blue plastic cup out of the cabinet, then a knife and spoon from the silverware drawer. If I were having avocado, that would require an additional knife, but not today. I put the cup next to the blender and the plate next to the toaster oven.

The toast goes in the toaster oven and I turn the dial an inch to the right, then open the refrigerator. A hard boiled egg goes on the plate.

Almond milk or coconut milk is the next decision. We're out of almond milk so no choice today. A dab of saved coffee added and its time to turn to the powders. First moringa, then cacao, then protein go into the blender container with the liquids.

I open the freezer. Blueberries (about a handful) and one and a half bananas are added, then filtered water up to a certain line on the container.

I turn off the toaster oven.

The top of the blender container goes on. I make sure the blender settings are on their lowest and turn on the blender, gradually increasing the speed. Then I flip the extra power toggle switch and count to thirty. Flipping it off, I gradually decrease the speed and turn it off, then pour the concoction into my blue plastic cup.

Opening the toaster oven, I turn the toast over, then turn it on again.

Time for vitamins. I open the drawer where I keep a week's worth in a separated holder and carefully open today's. One mouthful with the smoothie and then another. I pour the rest of the smoothie from the blender container into my cup and take it to my desk.

Fish food is in the pantry closet. I take it out, open the back porch door, and walk to the fish pond to be greeted by nine little mouths on the surface. I sprinkle the food and return to the kitchen.

Back at the toaster oven, I slice the egg in half and scoop it onto the plate. Salt is added, then pepper, then mixing it all together.

The toast is done. I turn the toaster oven off, unplug both it and the blender, then reach for my knife. Butter is applied to the toast evenly. No gaps. Each slice of toast is cut in half, then I scoop the egg onto each piece.

After rinsing out the blender container, I take the plate to my desk and begin the ritual of eating my breakfast.

DID I MAKE IT?

PROMPT: Did I make it ?

It was breathtakingly beautiful, we all agreed.

We also agreed that we had no idea what it was or where it had come from or what it was doing in the middle of Frank's cornfield.

And if asked, we would have disagreed on what was beautiful about it, although we couldn't know that. And wouldn't care.

Frank was the first to see it when he went out early in the morning to feed the chickens, who were strangely silent. Still half asleep, he usually kept his head down as he walked to the coop. Something drew his eyes to the field next to the barn.

Wow, he thought, then called into the house.

Martha, come on out here ! You've got to see this.

She was surprised to hear his voice. He rarely talked to her before the chores were complete, so she pulled on her threadbare robe and shuffled out the back door facing the field.

Wow, she thought.

What is it ? she said.

Frank shook his head.

I don't know, but it's beautiful, isn't it ?

Martha agreed.

I'm going to call Jim and Edna. They need to come over and see it, she said.

And that's how it started, until all of the townspeople were there, staring at the thing.

Downtown, the only activity was the street dogs scrounging for a meal amidst the trash, which was supposed to be picked up that morning. The trash collectors, along with everyone else, were out at Frank's farm, mesmerized by something they didn't understand, something that was so out of their mundane routines.

The mayor cleared his throat, attempting to get their attention and establish his authority. Everyone ignored him, so he spoke up.

Well, Frank, he said. That thing is certainly….beautiful. Did you make it ?

Did I make it ? Are you kidding ? Look at it. Does it look like something I could make ?

I don't know. It's in your cornfield.

No, I didn't make it. It was there when I went to feed the chickens this morning.

Ok. Well, I think it's time everyone gets on back to work.

Nobody moved.

It's so beautiful, someone said, and began to cry softly.

Downtown, the dogs, their bellies full, found comfortable places to sleep in the sun, undisturbed by humans. No car sounds disturbed their dreams. Shops stayed closed.

In the middle of Frank's cornfield, the bright shiny object remained, all eyes focused upon it.

The mayor considered making another attempt to rouse the people from whatever gripped them and get them back to their ordinary lives, then felt himself surrender to the beauty before him.

What the hell, he thought. It's so beautiful.

SOMEDAY

Prompt: Someday

Let's play a game!

His voice penetrated the haze of our collective altered consciousness. Some of us looked up, trying to make sense of his words. Others ignored him, caught up in various alternative realities that were more compelling.

I said, let's play a game !

This time he demanded our attention in that magnetic way we knew well, and all eyes turned toward him.

His demeanor softened. I recognized how he would now invite us into his agenda in a way that would be both welcoming and manipulative.

He paused, probably for dramatic effect, and said in a soft voice.

I love you, and I think it's time for us to deepen our sacred connection.

Was he looking at me ? Maybe. And probably everyone else present felt the same way.

I felt my energy shift, surrendering my individual exploration and its isolation, to the possibility that would emerge from engaging with the others in the room.

Someone broke the silence.

What kind of game ?

I'm glad you asked, he said with a laugh meant to ease the tension.

It is no accident that we've all gathered here, in this time and place, opening ourselves to the deep wisdom of our unseen allies. And if we just continued as we have been, I'm sure many of you will have an experience that will further your evolution.

I see another possibility, he said, and paused again, waiting for his words to land and knowing we would want more. We always did.

When he felt our desire, he leaned forward.

Let's play a game that will change our lives.

What a master he was ! It was certainly a cliché, and yet the way he expressed it sounded like absolute truth. Although I, and most if not all of the others, would say we were already committed to a life of change, all of that dissolved in this moment. As usual, he touched the deep unquenchable thirst in us and we eagerly approached the trough of his unique bounty, ready for whatever he was offering.

Someday...., he said.

We waited.

Someday...

****

Drew ? I heard a voice call my name. Drew, are you ok ?

I opened my eyes.

You were hardly breathing, and I was worried ?

I'm ok, I said, trying to remember something that felt important.

Good. The others are ready for you now.

107

I arose, went into the bathroom to wash my face, and looked into the mirror.

Showtime, I thought.

When I entered the room, I looked around.

Let's play a game, I said.

NEXT IDEA

PROMPT: Next idea

Nothing I'm thinking of writing seems inspiring. What will I do ? I'm here, and need to write something. Next idea is the prompt. I don't like it. Does it really matter whether I like it or not ? Just keep your fingers moving and eventually, maybe, something will emerge.

Something ? I'm waiting. Nothing is showing up. Is that possible ? How can nothing show up ? Nothing is something, isn't it ?

I remember the pen name I gave myself when I was doing morning pages every day, 3 pages to complete regardless of content. Or is it irregardless ? Anyway, I named myself Trite Drivel. Hi, Trite. Here you are again. Knock yourself out.

Oh well, who cares whether what I write today is trite or stupid or incoherent or anything else.

But, but….maybe I care.

OK. On to the next idea.

Uh. I don't have one.

Just keep writing.

You call this writing ?

Just keep your fingers moving. It really doesn't matter. In the long run, we're all dead, said the economist Keynes.

Death. That could be the next idea.

Nah. Reach for a better feeling thought, says the new age channel

Abraham, while you're paying me the big bucks for my courses.

Cynical ? A tad.

Up to 200 words, we are, with a half hour to go.

Having fun ? Sort of.

Just be and surrender to the next idea.

Who said that ?

The God within you, which is you.

Yeah, right. Sounds good, but how exactly do I do that ?

You don't do anything.

So I do nothing ? Isn't nothing something ?

Ah….you've looped back a few lines. Maybe it keeps coming back to that. What is the nature of nothing ?

Is that the next idea ? Wow, that's profound.

Tsk tsk. Looping back to cynical, are we ?

You're starting to sound like Yoda.

Am I ?

Now I'm back in about 1978, after going to see Star Wars 7 times. And a year later, I'm playing poker in Reno when a kid across the table asks me how many times I've seen Star Wars. A lot, I say. I thought so, he says.

A little while later, I'm walking across the casino and a woman says to me, "Mr. Lucas ?" No, I say, and walk on.

Back at the table, the kid comes over to me and asks for my autograph, telling me he loves my movie. Now I get it. OK, I'll play along with this, and sign "To another science fiction fan. Yours, George Lucas."

He asks if I will come to the restaurant where he works for a drink later and I say, "maybe".

When he leaves, one of the other players says, "yeah. I heard you were some big movie producer." The truth is that I'm just a 32 year old guy making a marginal living playing poker, waiting for the next idea.

That night I tell my girlfriend what happened. She laughs and shows me the latest Time Magazine with a story about George Lucas. There is a picture of him and surprise......it does look like me.

End of story. Except when it pops up from somewhere in my brain's warehouse of memories.

The next idea.....I'd like a new one, not from the warehouse. Most of those are obsolete.

So where will it come from, if not from all that's familiar ?

Just be, and trust. Surrender to the yet unknown, you must.

Thanks, Yoda. I'll let you know how it goes.

FEAR

Prompt: Fear

She had always been interesting to be around. I wondered what the topic of conversation would be today. After we were shown to our table, sat down and ordered, she jumped right in.

What are you afraid of ?

Nothing that I'm aware of right now.

I could see that she didn't believe me, and wondered if she was going to push it.

I didn't have to wonder very long.

Come on, she said. Everybody is afraid of something. Like right now, for instance. Don't you hear all that buzzing ? Those bees could attack us at any moment.

Possibly, but I doubt it. How's your book progressing ? You're writing about modern Mexico, aren't you ?

Don't change the subject, she said. What are you afraid of ?

If I didn't come up with something this was going to be a long lunch.

Physical pain, I said. I don't fear dying and death, at least theoretically, but I don't want to suffer physical pain.

She appeared satisfied at my answer, and I thought I was off the hook, until she said, "What else ?"

Why are you focusing so much on fear ? I asked. Some say it is an artifact from our most primitive brain, a survival mechanism. But there's little to fear these days. No saber tooth tiger is going to jump out of the bushes and eat you. Fear.....f e a r....stands for false expectations appearing real.

Are you kidding ? Little to fear ? False expectations ? Don't you follow the news ? I mean, it's a little better since trump is no longer president, but there are lots of reasons to be afraid.....covid, vaccines, fires, hurricanes, floods, and on and on and on.

I sighed. Maybe this would be a short lunch after all, if I could find an excuse to leave.

And don't forget the cartels ? More bodies were found this week near Guadalajara, chopped into pieces. I've been doing more research for my book and discovering stuff people need to know. Believe me, no one is safe.

Now I paused, choosing my words carefully.

Maybe, maybe not. I think we're safe if we keep our noses out of their business.

You mean we should do nothing and let innocent people die ?

Innocent people die all the time, from all sorts of causes. I think you should leave it alone.

I can't do that. She said vehemently.

OK. I appreciate your passion. The food's here. Can we just enjoy our lunch now, and not talk about fear or bees or death or the cartel ?

It was quiet while we ate. The meal finished and the check paid, I walked her to her car. We hugged and parted. She said, I'm sorry I was so intense. Let's get together again soon. Please ?

I agreed.

As I approached my car, I saw that there was someone in the passenger seat. Taking a deep breath, I opened the door and sat down.

Well ? he said.

She won't stop. Do what you have to do.

I HATE BEING LATE

Prompt: I hate being late

I hate being late. And I used to hate waiting for people who are late. Then I discovered the secret that changed my life.

My research unearthed the definition of waiting...."doing nothing in anticipation of a future event".

Why would I ever want to do that ?

So I decided that I would never, ever wait again, and came up with several alternatives to doing nothing in anticipation of a future event.

The one that has served me best is ABAB, which stands for "always bring a book". For example, if I'm sitting in the car, and my wife is inside the store taking whatever time she needs to shop for whatever it is she's shopping for, it doesn't bother me anymore......I have a book to read. No problem, honey. Take as much time as you want.

Fantasizing is another way of dealing with situations I would ordinarily be frustrated with. Sometimes it can be negative fantasizing about what I'd like to do to the person in front of me who is so obviously incompetent at their job and/or oblivious to how important what I immediately want is and how they should make what I want a priority.

Often it is simply more salacious fantasizing. And that's all I'll say about that.

A third alternative to waiting is perhaps the most radical. It is the practice of Being, simply breathing and experiencing all that is around me in the present moment, starting with myself. Tuning into my body

118

sensations and the space I take up. Opening all my senses to whatever I see, hear, smell, and feel. Observing and experiencing without judgment reality here and now.

There is nothing to wait for, ever.

A BABY'S SMILE

Prompt: a baby's smile

Is everyone here ?

The sound of Carole's voice reminded me that I was not alone. I looked around, not surprised to see that the room was full,

Deep inside myself, I had lost track of everything else, as was often the case these days. Today was not my day, but it was rapidly approaching.

A few deep breaths brought me back to the present moment, along with anticipation at what was about to happen.

Thank you all for coming, she said. Brenda, would you join me, please ?

A short, round-faced woman rose and began to stride up to the front of the room, carrying a bundle in her arms. Her face showed no expression.

The others watched her in silence. No one moved.

Carole motioned her to stand next to her, facing the rest of us.

Carole's eyes closed.

I felt a visceral shift in the energy of the room, as if some ancient forces were gathering, adding to our collective field.

The silence felt thick and timeless.

Carole's eyes opened and she reached her arms toward Brenda.

Now, she said.

Brenda held out the bundle and began to unwrap the blankets surrounding what lay inside, until the naked infant was fully exposed.

Carole reached for the baby, cradling it gently as she gazed lovingly at it.

Then her expression abruptly changed and when she spoke it was a different voice we heard, a voice that contained countless generations of child-bearing women, inviting and imploring us with their ancient message.

"We hold Life in our hands. May we always remember that although we are merely the vessels for Life to continue, it is our sacred duty to nurture, love and cherish our offspring while they are helpless and dependent on us. And then we must release them to their own destiny. Each new being does not belong to us alone, but to the greater community of humanity. May they find their purpose and contribute to the good of all, in service to the continuing evolution of Life on this planet. May they choose wisely as they face the challenges of living in this physical form and reality."

She held the baby toward us.

"I invite you to welcome this new being into our hearts and lives."

I and all the others in the room focused our total attention on the baby. The energy in the room became like a harmonic chord of acceptance and built to a powerful, yet gentle vibration that was palpable.

The baby smiled.

I put my hands on my rapidly growing belly, joyful in knowing the welcome my little one would receive when they arrived.

BUT HE'S MY FATHER

Prompt: but he's my father

The obituary was beautifully written. I received many emails telling me that. At least three. And one person even called to offer me condolences. I made a mental note to thank the writer I had hired to do the job.

It was a good thing I hadn't ordered food for the sitting at home. No one showed up. Not even my brother.

My wife had the good sense to leave me alone. She went to visit her mother the day we heard about my father's death.

My dog sat at my feet in the living room, probably unaware of the circumstances and not caring.

I dozed for awhile, then awoke. Disoriented, then remembering.

Early memories were hazy. He was gone a lot, leaving my brother and me with our mother. She made sure we were fed and clothed, but not much else. As I got older and became involved in sports, he seemed to show up more. A picture shows both of us in baseball uniforms. I'm about 11 years old. Was he the coach of the team ? Maybe.

When I reached my teens, golf became my passion. Instead of going to the beach with friends on weekends, I played with mom and dad, improving quickly. He was an above average golfer and by the time I was 15 I was better. He actually seemed to like that, and enjoyed my tournament successes.

We began to spend more time alone. And that's when things changed. Especially when he introduced me to his girlfriend.

It was confusing and also perversely bonding. We had a secret ! And as I began my adolescent rebellion to my mother's limited view of right and wrong, he was my ally, using me to vent about her and justify his actions. She became our common enemy.

Decades passed. He remained on the pedestal he had supplied the materials for me to build. The family system stayed intact.

Until I began to explore what made me tick, going through a variety of psychological experiences and therapies that led me to the Hoffman Process, a deep dive into early childhood influences.

It was shocking to discover. My story about who I was shattered, finally, in a good way. The filters through which I experienced myself, my parents, and the world, which I never knew were there, dropped away and a new clarity revealed itself.

My perfect father, my hero, my role model.......was not such a good guy.

My mother was not as bad as my father had made her out to be.

And me ? My own self image, the identity I had worked so hard to present to the world, turned out to be more malleable than I had thought.

My relationship with my mother changed instantly, as I saw her in a new way, and was able to accept her and love her. She didn't understand what had happened, but enjoyed the connection we were able to have until she died seven years later.

It was different with my father. Things were strained when I stopped colluding with him. It took several years to find a different level for us to relate. After my mother died, he entered another relationship almost immediately with someone he had known for over sixty years, the widow of his best friend. Had they been lovers before ?, I wondered.

They were together over twenty years before he died.

And now I sat alone, reviewing the journey I had been on as the son of my parents.

The week after his death, I received a condolence email from a cousin I hadn't seen in close to fifty years, daughter of my father's sister. She expressed support for me and said there was something she needed to talk to me about.

In a phone call the following week, she told me he had molested her when she was fifteen years old. I was shocked, but not totally surprised.

From "he's not such a good guy", my memory of him turned to "he was a bad guy" for a year and a half, until I was able to release all fixed definitions of him. And felt free, able to hold him as a flawed human being.

He can be judged in any number of ways for his actions. But in the end, the fact remains he was my father.

I COULDN'T STOP LAUGHING

Prompt: I couldn't stop laughing

I'm serious, she said, looking very serious.

I know, I said, hoping my face showed the appropriate expression.

Really, she insisted, I'm really serious this time.

Ok.

I leaned forward.

I know what you're doing, she said, her eyes squinting. It's what you do when you're patronizing me.

I leaned back.

Honey, that's not what I'm doing. I know this is important to you and I want to make sure I understand.

She leaned forward.

So tell me what you heard me say.

I took a deep breath.

You think this is all my fault and you're perfect and have no responsibility for anything that is stressful in our relationship, I thought, and quickly realized it would probably not be a good thing to say.

I heard you say that you feel alone and unpartnered when I'm defensive and argumentative and that you want me to work on my reactivity and projection.

She seemed to relax a little.

I leaned forward.

What else ? she said.

I leaned back.

What did I miss ? I said.

She looked at me for an hour or two and didn't say anything. At least that's how it felt.

I don't know what you want me to say. I said in what I hoped sounded like a calm and vulnerable tone.

Her expression changed in a familiar way. I braced for impact.

What do you want to say ?

Several answers instantly came to mind, all of which would likely lead me to packing my bags and finding another place to live. I let them pass and considered other options.

I really love you and hate when we get into something like this. I want to be a better partner and husband. I'm sorry for anything and everything I've done that has caused you pain and made you want to distance from me.

Her expression changed again.

Are you sure ? she said, suspiciously.

Yes, I said firmly, I've never been so sure of something in my life.

CUT !, yelled the director. Good work.

Brenda and I took a deep breath, looked at each other, and simultaneously broke into laughter that seemed like it wouldn't stop.

When it finally subsided, she said. That was fun, wasn't it ?

Just like old times, I said, and we both began to laugh again.

I love you, she said.

I love you, too, I responded, and took her into my arms.

OK. Next scene, said the director.

The Artist's Creed

I am worth the time it takes to create whatever I feel called to create. The time I spend creating is precious, a valuable expression of my aliveness and vitality.

My work is worthy of its own space, which is Sacred. When I enter this space, I have the right to work in silence, uninterrupted, for as long as I choose, without allowing myself to be distracted.

The moment I open myself to the gifts of the Muse, I open myself to The Source of all Creation. I am not alone in my attempts to create.

What it is I am called to do will make itself known when I have made myself ready and fully engage. My work is joyful and constantly changing, flowing through me with ease.

What truly matters in the making of my art is not what the final piece looks or sounds like, not what it is worth or not worth. What matters is the newness added to the universe in the process of creating the piece itself.

Once I begin the work, the words or sounds will take shape, the form find life, and Spirit takes flight.

As the Muse gives to me, so does she deserve from me: faith, mindfulness, and enduring commitment.

---Adapted from Jan Phillips "Marry Your Muse"

Other Resources

https://writingexercises.co.uk/index.php

https://thewritespot.us/marlenecullenblog/category/prompts/

https://lauradavis.net/the-writers-journey/

www.writingretreats.org

Other Prompts

It's only a game

Something went wrong

Overheard from the next table

It could be worse

Scary but interesting

The steam bubbled up

My beloved car

It was her hat that caught his attention

It's how we do things around here

OK, give me proof

Unsolicited advice

Don't back up

Taken into custody

What I might have done, but didn't

Why didn't you call me ?

It was the last good day

I remember the smell of _____

My mother never told me

You opened my letter

Who is fooling whom ?

I forgot

Sidetracked

Is anyone listening ?

And the singers sang

Too much information

My pal

Made in United States
Orlando, FL
10 June 2025

62019342R00085